M000195392

Get Back

Get Back

12 Short Stories

by

Don Tassone

Golden Antelope Press
715 E. McPherson
Kirksville, Missouri 63501
2017

Copyright ©2017 by Don Tassone

All rights reserved. No portion of this publication may be dupli-
cated in any way without the expressed written consent of the pub-
lisher, except in the form of brief excerpts or quotations for review
purposes.

ISBN   978-1-936135-28-8 (1-936135-28-0)

Library of Congress Control Number: 2017935232

Published by:
Golden Antelope Press
715 E. McPherson
Kirksville, Missouri 63501

Available at:
Golden Antelope Press
715 E. McPherson
Kirksville, Missouri, 63501
Phone: (660) 665-0273
http://www.goldenantelope.com
Email: ndelmoni@gmail.com

"Get back to where you once belonged."
— Paul McCartney

Acknowlegments:

These stories, in earlier versions, were first published elsewhere. Grateful acknowledgment to the editors of these literary magazines.

- *101 Words*: "The Red Wagon."
- *Olentangy Review*: "The Beauty in Things."
- *Ray's Road Review*: "Who is Peter Caruso?"
- *Red Fez*: "Free."
- *Sick Lit Magazine*: "Forbidden Fruit," "The Pin Insulator," and "The Box."
- *Story Shack*: "The Pin Insulator" and "Hold On."
- *TreeHouse*: "Hold On."
- *TWJ Magazine*: "The Clearing," "Street Ball and Joe's Red Bike," and "The Test."
- *The Zodiac Review*: "Unplugged."

Contents

The Red Wagon

When he was a boy, he had a red wagon. His earliest memories were of his mother pulling him down the sidewalk.

He remembered the little thump caused by each seam of the sidewalk. He remembered his mother giving him a box of animal crackers for the ride. He remembered coming home, where she would give him a glass of cold milk.

Now his life is hard. But on his toughest days, when he might go mad, he closes his eyes and holds on to the sides of his red wagon, feeling the bumps on the sidewalk and going home again.

The Beauty in Things

Roasted verlasso salmon. Piquillo pepper sauce, broccoli, red-skin potatoes, horse radish sour crème. $23.

It was the first entrée that caught his eye on the menu, which was posted on the window. He was trying to cut back on red meat. But he was too hungry to go vegetarian tonight. So salmon sounded perfect. And at $23, he knew he could still have a glass of wine and not bust his expense account. After so many meals on the road, he could do the math in his head.

He pulled open the heavy oak door. The warm air and the scent and sound of sizzling steak drew him inside.

"Welcome to Julian's!" said the hostess, sounding cordial but not really paying attention.

"Do you have a reservation?" she asked as she busily crossed names off the waiting list.

"Good evening," he said. "No, I don't. Do I need one?"

"No," said the hostess. "I just like to check. Will someone be joining you this evening?"

"No," he said quietly. "Just one."

Finally, she looked up. He was as handsome as he was unassuming, and he now had her full attention.

"Very good," she said softly.

He traveled a couple of days a week, almost always alone. But he had never gotten used to sitting at a table by himself. It made him feel awkward.

"Do you serve dinner at the bar?" he asked.

"Yes, of course."

His eyes scanned the restaurant, looking for the bar. But he didn't see one.

"Right this way, sir," said the hostess.

He followed her through the restaurant. The bar was in the back. They walked by a ladies-night-out table. Several of the women stopped chatting and looked up as he passed. He looked away, as if he didn't notice. But he did notice. He had simply grown used to it.

"Will there be anything else?" asked the hostess.

"No," he said. "Thank you."

"Enjoy your dinner," she said, lingering for a moment, watching him as he made his way to the bar.

The room was dark and cozy, with just enough space for three tall tables. People were having dinner at two of them. A fire crackled in a stone fireplace, which took up much of one wall. The bar itself was short, with only three stools, all empty. They were the kind with backs, which he liked.

He didn't drink much, but he liked bars. He appreciated their clean lines and vibrant colors. His favorites were the ones where the liquor and wine bottles were carefully arranged on glass shelves and backlit.

This bar was like that. There were two shelves against the back wall. On each was a mosaic of bottles, varied by color and height. He stood back for a moment to take it in, as an art lover might study a painting.

"Good evening, sir," said the bartender. "May I start you out with a drink?"

"Good evening," he said, saddling up to the stool on the right. He was always careful to leave enough space for others.

"Actually," he said, "I'd like to go ahead and order dinner."

"Very good," said the bartender. "Would you like to see a menu?"

"No, thanks. I was looking at your menu outside. I think I'll have the salmon and a glass of your house chardonnay."

"Excellent choice. Anything else? A cocktail before dinner?"

"No, thanks. But I will take the wine, please, whenever you're ready."

"Very good. Let me place your order, and I'll have your wine in just a moment."

He felt the warmth from the fire on his back and realized he was still wearing his coat. He stood up to take it off, looked around and spotted a coat rack in the corner. He went over and hung up his coat.

He was walking back to the bar when he saw someone come in from the restaurant. It was the hostess, followed by a woman.

"Here we are," said the hostess, looking his way. "It looks like we have one open table and, of course, the bar."

"Thank you," said the woman, as the hostess took one last glance, then disappeared.

He wondered if the woman might come over to the bar, but he didn't want to stare. So he sat back down.

His glass of wine was waiting. He took a sip and looked up. Once again, the colorful bottles caught his eye. But now, looking more carefully, he realized there was a mirror behind them. In it, in a space between the rows of bottles, he could see the reflection of the woman who had just come in.

She was still standing in the doorway, looking around the room. Then she walked over to the hearth. She held her hands up to the fire and rubbed them together slowly.

She was tall and thin, with long, brown hair. She wore a dark blue coat and a white scarf. He couldn't get a good look at her face. But he guessed she was in her mid-thirties, like him.

Watching her in the mirror, he began to feel a bit voyeuristic, so he looked down at his glass of wine. But a few moments later, hearing footsteps behind him, he glanced back up. In the mirror, he saw her approaching the stool to his far left.

"Do you mind if I sit here?" she asked.

"No," he said, pivoting slightly to face her. She was quite plain-looking. "Not at all."

"Thanks," she said.

She took off her scarf and coat, then hesitated, not knowing exactly where to put them.

"There's a coat rack in the corner," he said, nodding toward it. He thought about offering to hang up her coat, but that felt too forward.

"Thanks," she said.

He watched her as she walked to the coat rack but faced forward as she turned around to walk back to the bar. She passed behind him and hitched herself up on the stool, leaving one seat between them.

"Good evening, miss," said the bartender. "May I start you out with a drink tonight?"

"Yes," she said, glancing at his wine. "I'd like a glass of your house cabernet, please."

"Very good. Would you like to see a menu?"

"No, thanks. I saw it out front. I think I'll go ahead and order dinner."

She looked over at him, as if to make sure that would be okay.

"By all means," he said. "I've just ordered dinner myself."

"Then I'd like the filet mignon," she said, "medium rare, with a baked potato and mixed vegetables."

"Sour cream?"

"Yes, please."

"Very good," he said. "I'll be right back with your wine, miss, and some fresh bread for each of you."

Fresh bread. Please hurry, he thought. After hearing "filet mignon," he was suddenly feeling famished—and a little wimpy for ordering the salmon.

He turned to her.

"My name is Michael," he said, smiling and extending his hand.

"Hi, Michael," she said. "I'm Sarah."

Her hand was thin, but her grip was surprisingly strong. She held his hand tightly and didn't let go right away, causing him to face her a moment longer. He looked into her face. It was as plain as winter wheat. But not for long because her eyes, which sparkled like emeralds, lit it up. They made it lovely. It was as if her face were a blank canvas on which some unseen artist was just beginning to work.

The part of him which did not like to stare gave way to the part which was drawn to the beauty in the most ordinary things. And so, for a moment, he looked into her eyes. He could not avert his gaze. Nor did he want to.

She took the fact that he was staring at her as license to study him: his olive skin, his blue eyes, his strong jaw, his cheeks and chin covered with stubble, his black hair, combed back, falling down to his shoulders, curling at his neck.

"Here you are, miss," said the bartender, setting down her glass of wine. "Enjoy."

With that, at last, she released her grip. He let go too, and they both swiveled back toward the bar.

"Cheers," he said, raising his glass.

"Cheers," she said, grateful for the opportunity to see his face again.

She watched him take a drink. He was not wearing a ring.

"So what brings you here?" he asked.

"Business," she said. "I'm here on business."

"Me too."

"I'm visiting customers."

"So am I."

"What do you do?" she asked.

"I'm sort of in the furniture business."

"Sort of?"

"Well, yes. I'm in the office furniture business."

She frowned ever so slightly. He wasn't sure if she was more curious or less.

"I'm a designer," he added. "I work with high-end clients to design executive offices."

"Sounds interesting," she said, sounding relieved.

"It is, most of the time."

"Most of the time?"

"Well," he said, smiling, "when my clients let me design."

This time, she didn't ask for clarification. She simply smiled and tilted her head, as if to say go on.

"I mean my clients are very successful," he said. "But they're business people. They're not designers. That's where I come in. When they let me design, when they take me seriously, I do my best work."

He looked down at his wine glass, squeezing the stem between his fingertips. What am I doing? he thought. All she did was ask me what I do.

"When they take you seriously?" she asked.

"Yeah."

"Why wouldn't your clients take you seriously?"

"Some people," he said, deciding to roll with it, "tend to judge a book by its cover."

"What do you mean?"

"Some of my customers, at least at first, see me as a lightweight."

"A lightweight?"

"A pretty boy."

"Oh."

"They're wrong, of course," he said. He didn't mean to sound so defensive. "I mean they're mistaken about me being a lightweight."

"How do you convince them you're not?"

He looked up to see if she was really interested. He couldn't tell. But then again, he could never tell for sure.

"Through my work," he said. "I show them what I can do."

"I see."

"Dinner is served," said the bartender, returning with both their plates. He set hers down, then his. Michael looked at his salmon, then over at her steak. He really needed to get off this diet.

"What about you?" he asked. "What do you do?"

"I'm an IT specialist," she said. "Essentially, I'm a troubleshooter. My company sends me out to help customers solve big computer problems, the ones we can't handle over the phone or online."

"So, do you travel a lot?"

"Yeah, a lot," she said. "Too much really."

"You don't like to travel?"

"It's okay. It's just that ..."

"What?"

"It's just that I really like working with computers, but I'm not crazy about working with people."

Now it was his turn to simply smile and tilt his head.

"I love math," she explained. "That's how I got into computers."

"That's cool," he said. "What is it you love about math?"

She paused, as if she were wondering how much to share.

"Some people are put off by math," she said. "But I've always loved numbers. I know it might sound crazy, but there is something about numbers that I find very appealing."

"What do you think that is?" he asked.

"I'm not sure. But I think it has something to do with being so authentic."

"So authentic?"

"I mean numbers are just what they are. A four is a four. It will never be a five. And it makes no apologies for being a four."

He grinned.

"Well," she said. "It's as unapologetic as a number can be."

He laughed.

"I like numbers because they're real," she said. "They're solid. You can rely on them. And I'm drawn to that."

"You mean you can count on them?"

She laughed loudly at his pun. Seeing her laugh made him laugh too.

"So how did you get into computers?"

"Well, for a while, I thought about teaching math," she said. "I even did some tutoring in college. But I'm just not very good with people. So I went into computers. That way, I thought I could focus on math and not have worry too much about people. But as it turns out, working with people is now a big part of my job."

"If you don't mind me asking," he said, "why don't you like working with people?"

"I like people," she said. "But to most people I work with, I'm just a computer geek. I'm there to fix their problems. And then I move on, and I never hear from them again. After a while, it makes you feel like just another part of the service contract."

"I see," he said. "I'm sorry."

She tilted back on her stool, away from him. He sensed she was suddenly uneasy.

"Thank you for sharing that," he said. "I know exactly what you mean."

"You do?" she smiled, leaning back toward him.

"Yeah. All my life, I've felt people were looking past me. They see me on the outside, and they form conclusions. But hardly anyone takes the time to get to know me. I mean the real me. No one ever asks me what I think."

"I know what you mean."

"You do?"

"Yes, I do," she said, "because no one ever asks me how I feel."

For a moment, they sat in silence.

"It kind of makes you feel one-dimensional, doesn't it?" he asked.

"Yeah," she said. "That's a good way to put it."

"But the good news," he said, trying to lighten things up again, "is that you found a way to do what you love. Math, I mean."

"Yeah," she said, smiling. "I guess you're right. I do get to work with numbers every day."

"How is your food, folks?" asked the bartender. They looked down at their plates. They hadn't eaten much.

"Good," Michael lied. His salmon was as bland as tapioca.

"You've barely touched your salmon," the bartender said to him. "Is it okay?"

"It's fine. But next time," he said with a smile, "I'm going with the filet."

"Would you like me to exchange it?" asked the bartender.

"No, thanks," he said. "But I'd love another glass of wine. How about you, Sarah?"

"Sure."

She picked up her knife and fork and cut her filet in half. She rested her knife on the edge of her plate and speared one half of the filet with her fork.

"Please take some of mine," she said, reaching out and holding the beef a few inches from his plate. "I could never eat it all anyway."

He noticed her hand was shaking.

"Thank you," he said, picking up his plate and setting it down between them. He placed his left hand on her hand to steady it. With his right, he slid the beef off of her fork and onto his plate.

"Will you make mine a cab too?" he called to the bartender.

"Very good," he said.

"So tell me, Sarah," eagerly cutting into the filet. "Have you always loved math?"

"Always," she said, "even as a girl. Of course, that didn't make me very popular. None of the other girls seemed to care much for math, and boys didn't tend to go crazy over math geeks."

He smiled. "Well, that's changed a lot."

"I sure hope so."

"Well, I'm sure the boys eventually came around."

"Not really."

"Oh, come on," he said. "Surely you had guys after you."

"Not one," she said, shaking her head.

"You mean you didn't date in school?"

"Not at all."

He looked over to make sure she wasn't kidding. A certain sadness in her face told him she was telling the truth.

"There are a lot of good guys out there," he said.

"Yeah, there are, and I've been interested in some of them. But none has been interested in me."

The bartender was back with their wine.

"May I take your plates?" he asked.

"Sure," he said.

"Yes, please," she added.

"Will there be anything else right now?"

"No, thanks," they said in unison. The bartender took the hint and retreated to the kitchen.

"You just haven't met the right guy yet," Michael said quietly. "I mean somebody who can see the real you."

She looked at him, smiled and took a sip of wine.

"What about you?" she asked. "Tell me about you."

"What would you like to know?"

"Tell me why a designer is in the office furniture business."

"You really want to know?" he asked, smiling.

"Are you kidding? I just told you I'm a math geek and I've never had a date. Bring it on."

"When I was a kid," he said, "I wanted to be an artist. I guess my parents spotted some talent in me because, when I was only six, they signed me up for art lessons and bought me a bunch of art supplies. They even set up a little studio for me in our den. I used to spend hours and hours drawing and painting in there."

"What did you draw?"

"Well, I pretty much drew the everyday things around me—a chair, a desk, a TV, a lamp, a filing cabinet, books on bookshelves. I even drew my sister, my brother and my dog, although none of them would sit very still."

She laughed at the thought of his dog sitting for a portrait. He was glad to know she was still paying attention.

"We had a long, sliding glass window with a thin marble sill in that room," he continued. "My mother put five crystal decanters along the sill. She filled them with water and added a few drops of food coloring. Red, green, blue, yellow and purple. And when the sunlight streamed in through the window, they looked like a rainbow. I sat there and looked at those decanters, and the way the light came through them, for hours. And I painted them dozens of times. They were my favorite things to paint. And they were always a challenge because the light and the colors were always changing."

"That sounds so lovely," she said.

"Well, that's just it. My art teacher had a very different idea of beauty. She wanted me to do mountains and sunsets and windmills. But to me, the ordinary things around me were the real things of beauty, the true objects of art."

"So what did you do?"

"Well, my teacher was pretty stubborn—and persuasive. She convinced my parents I should 'broaden my horizons.' So I began drawing mountain ranges and windmills—things I'd never even seen."

"Did you like it?"

"No! I hated it. But I did it. I painted those things for my teacher and my parents. But I kept painting desks and chairs and those decanters too. I hid that work in a big box I kept in my closet."

"Did your parents ever find out?"

"No," he said. "They had no clue. In fact, they were so thrilled with my landscapes that they sent me to art school for college."

"How was that?"

"Initially, awful. But over time, great because I got exposed to interior design, which I loved. And when I graduated, I went to work designing offices."

"So you stuck with it too?" she asked.

"Yeah," he said. "Except, of course, for a little side trip to learn how to draw mountains."

He smiled and looked at her.

"You found a way to do what you've always loved," she said.

"Yeah."

He looked up at the bottles on the shelves behind the bar. The colors sparkled in the reflection of the flicker of the flames from the fireplace.

Then he looked back over at her. The fire danced in her eyes. Now, though, they weren't just green. Now they were alive with the color from every bottle. And suddenly her face, though still plain, looked so very elegant. It was transformed, not by the bottles or even her eyes, but by a light from within.

He drew a breath and blinked.

"Sarah?"

"Yeah?"

"Have you ever had your portrait painted?"

She gave him a quizzical look.

"No," she said. "I haven't."

"Would you be open to it?"

"Yeah, I guess."

"Are you still in town tomorrow evening?"

"Yes."

"Great," he said. "Then let's get together tomorrow. I'll bring my sketch book."

"Really?"

"Yeah, really," he said, smiling and raising his glass. "It's a date."

Who is Peter Caruso?

His alarm went off, as usual, at 5:00 a.m. Five minutes earlier, his Bodum Bistro coffeemaker had clicked on and begun brewing two cups of aged Sumatran coffee. By the time he went to the bathroom and got to the kitchen, the air was heavy with the aroma of burnt spice.

He poured the first cup into a black ceramic mug. The thermal carafe would keep the second cup hot until he was ready for it, after he worked out, in ninety minutes. He would sip it on his way to work.

Now, though, he made his way back down the hallway to his study. The room was dark. He reached inside the doorway and felt along the rough, brick wall until his fingertips bumped into a wooden switch plate. He flipped the switch, and a lamp on his desk filled the room with pale yellow light. He stepped onto the plush oriental rug, soft and warm on his bare feet, sat down in the high-back leather chair and logged on to his computer.

Then, as he did every morning, he Googled his name, Peter Caruso. As he waited for the search results, he picked up a pencil on his desk and began doodling on a scratch pad. "Who is Peter Caruso?" he scribbled.

Up popped three news stories, two analyst reports and one blog. They had all been posted overnight. He sipped his coffee and leaned in for a closer look.

It was all the result of a presentation he had made at an investor conference the day before. There, he had challenged his fellow investment advisers to "double down" on value investing by "buying far more cheap stocks, then not hesitating to unload them."

And to support his case, he announced that, by following this strategy, many of his clients were now seeing a 20% return on their investments, more than twice the market average, after only two years.

During the Q&A session, he got plenty of push back, just as he expected. His lively back-and-forth with several investors, and his refusal to divulge his "proprietary formulas" for determining the best "cheap stocks" and when to sell, made for some colorful quotes and good copy.

He knew how to make news. His firm, Taft and Irving, knew that too. Whenever they needed some good PR, they turned to Peter.

And he delivered superbly, making a name for himself in the process. In financial circles, he had become a celebrity. Analysts, investors, journalists—they all wanted to talk with Peter Caruso.

This star quality, and his ability to use it to bring in big-money clients, made Peter one of Taft and Irving's most valuable assets. No wonder he made partner at thirty-two. No wonder he was now rumored to be a CEO contender.

He smiled, sat back in his chair and closed his eyes. He held his coffee mug in both hands, just under his chin, and breathed in the sweet, earthy aroma. The steam warmed the inside of his nose.

Then he opened his eyes and looked across the room at a large, cherry bookcase. It held dozens of books and an array of exotic objects he had collected from around the world: a white jade Buddha, a glazed ceramic vase, an intricately carved sandstone horse.

But now his eyes focused on a single piece, set back in the center of the bookcase, that was far less refined: a watercolor painting of a small, red-brick house. It was the house where he grew up. He had made that picture when he was six years old.

He remembered sitting in his front yard and sketching it, then going to his room and painting it with watercolors. He remembered how proud and excited he felt when his mother framed it and hung it on his bedroom wall.

It was the only piece in his apartment from his childhood, the only hint of a middle-class world on the twelfth floor of a luxury high-rise on the Upper West Side of Manhattan, the only inexpensive thing in the place.

And his eyes were focused on it now because he liked to be reminded of what it felt like to create something. He was no longer creating. Now his days were spent optimizing assets. That's what his life was about.

But his little painting was a reminder that that wasn't always the case and that long before he was collecting art, he was creating it.

Looking at it made him feel half-empty. It was a feeling he was having more and more, a feeling he could not seem to shake.

...

He walked to the door and was about to turn off the light. But he stopped and looked at the solid brick wall in front of him. It was so plain. But this morning there was something about it that made him pause. He reached out and ran his fingertips over it, then pressed the palm of his hand against it.

He closed his eyes and thought of the summer when he was fifteen, the summer he had worked with his father. His father was a bricklayer. It was just the two of them.

That was more than twenty-five years ago, and he no longer remembered the details. But he remembered the feeling of creating something real—a wall, a patio, a walkway—of working with something he could hold in his hands. He loved creating. He loved designing. He loved learning his father's art.

But Peter's body wasn't thick like his father's. He had inherited his mother's more slender build. And as much as he loved the art of working with brick, it was hard on his body.

Before that summer, Peter had pretty much decided he would go to college. By the end, any doubt was removed. He knew he could never do such physical work for a living. Maybe that was his father's aim all along.

Now, though, as he touched the rough surface of the wall, he realized how much he missed it. Not laying brick. But creating something real.

...

He stepped out of the shower, dried off and stepped onto his Fitbit scale. 157.8 pounds. Good, he thought. Still under one-sixty.

It was Friday. Some in his office had begun to dress casually on Fridays. But he would be seeing clients and always dressed to impress. So he picked out a dark blue Armani suit, a light blue Ferragamo tie and, as always, a freshly pressed, white cotton shirt.

He got dressed, then checked himself out in a floor-length mirror in his bedroom. The dark suit and light tie were an elegant combination. How could his clients not be impressed?

Back in his kitchen, he poured a bottle of water, a scoop of chocolate whey protein powder and a cup of frozen berries into his Vitamix blender, pressed the button for smoothie, poured it into a tall glass and drank it down.

Then he poured his second cup of coffee into a small, stainless steel travel mug, grabbed his iPhone and Maui Jims, shut his apartment door tight behind him and pressed the button for the elevator.

When he got to the lobby, the receptionist and door man, Robert, greeted him.

"Good morning, Mr. Caruso."

"Good morning, Robert."

"You're looking very sharp this morning."

"Well, thank you, Robert. I'm meeting with some high rollers today."

"How can they resist?"

Peter smiled. "That's what I'm banking on, Robert."

"My money's on you, Mr. Caruso," Robert said, as he opened the door for him.

The sun was just rising, and he put on his sunglasses. Robert scooted past him and opened the right rear door of a black Lincoln Town Car that was waiting at the curb.

"Thank you, Robert."

Then Peter pulled a tightly folded $100 bill from his right pants pocket.

"Have a great weekend, Robert," he said, discretely handing him the bill. Neither of the men looked down. But Peter looked around to see who might be watching. Sometimes, if someone was walking by, he would unfold the bill just a little and pause for a moment before handing it off.

"Give my best to Barbara."

"Thank you, Mr. Caruso. You have a wonderful weekend."

...

The fall air was crisp, but it was not yet cool enough for an overcoat. It was his favorite time of the year. He especially liked driving past Central Park when the leaves were turning. It reminded him of home.

"Good morning, Mr. Caruso," said his driver.

"Good morning, Charles."

"Beautiful morning. Would you like to drive through the park today?"

"That's very tempting, Charles. But I think I'll pass this morning. I'll be running there tomorrow, and I need to get ready for a meeting. But thanks."

"Very good," Charles said, taking the hint and giving it a little gas as he headed south toward Midtown.

Tomorrow would be fun. After running in the park in the morning, he would take in the new Matisse exhibition at the Museum of Modern Art. In the evening, he would get together at a dinner party with friends.

He had bought a new Cesare Attolini cashmere blazer and Bruno Magli shoes, just for the occasion. Trendy clothes had become his signature at these parties. And good wine. Tomorrow, he would bring a bottle of Sassicaia from Tuscany, a 2006 he had been saving.

Now he arrived at his office building. Charles got out, scurried around the front of the car and opened the door.

"Have a great day, Mr. Caruso."

"Thank you, Charles. I'll see you back here a little before noon."

...

Ariana, Taft and Irving's pretty and perennially upbeat receptionist, greeted him as he got off the elevator on the sixteenth floor.

"Good morning, Mr. Caruso," she said cheerfully, looking up from her computer. "And congratulations on all the good PR this morning!"

"Good morning, Ariana. Yes, I saw some of that myself. Do you really think it's okay?"

"Oh, yes. And the photos of you. Very fine."

"Thank you, Ariana," he said, smiling. "You've just made my day."

As he made his way to his office in the corner, several other colleagues congratulated him too. He acted modest. But inside, he was beaming.

"Good morning, Mr. Caruso," said his secretary, Pam. She was sitting in her cubicle, just outside his office. She had already been at work for more than an hour.

"Good morning, Pam."

"You're looking very elegant today."

"Well, thank you, Pam. It's a big day, you know."

He had only three appointments, but all with heavy hitters: one in the morning, one over lunch and one in the afternoon.

Their portfolios were quite different, and his proposals were carefully tailored. But his aim for all three was the same: to convince them to invest more. And if they bought what he was selling, he figured it would net him an extra hundred grand. Not a bad day.

"I've inserted a set of all the latest articles mentioning you in the front pocket of each of your binders," Pam said.

Three binders, each of them sporting the Taft and Irving logo, lay in a perfect row across a walnut credenza that ran along the window, perpendicular to his large, ebony desk. Next to each binder was slender file on that client. He liked to have all his materials for the day lined up there in the morning.

"Thank you, Pam. You're always a step ahead."

...

His first meeting could not have gone better. Now he was sitting at a table at Bellini, his second client's favorite place for lunch. The two of them were sipping bourbon, neat, and had just ordered food.

He was about to wrap up the small talk and begin his pitch when his phone began vibrating. Who on earth would be calling him now? During lunch, his business calls were automatically routed to Pam.

"Excuse me," he said, sliding his phone out of his jacket pocket and looking embarrassed.

"Of course."

He looked down at the caller's name. It was Maria, his sister.

"Hello?"

"Pete, it's Maria." She sounded upset.

"Maria, what's up?"

"It's dad."

"Dad?"

"He had another heart attack."

"Is he okay?"

"We're not sure."

"What do you mean?"

"He's in surgery."

"Where's mom?"

"She's here, with me, waiting at the hospital."

"Do you think I should come home?"

Silence.

"Maria, do you think I should come home?"

"Yes. Yes, Pete, I do."

"I'll leave as soon as I can."

"Okay."

"Tell Dad I'm on my way."

"Okay. I'll tell him."

...

"Nice suit."

Peter blinked. He had been staring out the window as the plane took off. Now he looked down and realized he was still wearing his suit.

"Thank you," he said to the man sitting next to him.

He had stopped by his apartment just long enough to pack a few things before heading to LaGuardia. He had been in such a rush that he forgot to change clothes.

Charles, who had been waiting at the restaurant, took him directly to his apartment. Peter called Pam on the way to fill her in and ask her to book him on the next flight to St. Louis.

After a quick stop at his apartment, Charles drove him directly to the airport. Uncharacteristically, Peter was silent the whole way.

When they arrived, he let himself out as Charles grabbed his carry-on bag from the trunk.

"Good luck, Mr. Caruso. My prayers are with you."

"Thank you, Charles."

Then he handed him a $100 bill. No one was watching. But he didn't care.

...

Now he had turned back to the window. He looked down at the ships along the Hudson and began thinking about his father.

His name was Dominic. He had come to the United States with his parents, Angelo and Rose, from Italy when he was eight.

Angelo was a bricklayer. No one in his family had ever left Italy. But the war had left his poor town even poorer, and he wanted a better life for Rose and Dominic, their only child. And so Angelo made what was, at that point, the biggest and toughest decision of his life: to leave his homeland for the U.S.

He had heard from friends that there were many Italians who had moved to a place called St. Louis. People were building a lot of houses there. And so in 1950, he sold everything he owned and struck out for St. Louis.

The three of them took a boat across the Mediterranean to Portugal and then a ship across the Atlantic to Ellis Island. From there, they took a ferry to Jersey City and, from there, trains to St. Louis. In all, the journey took them nearly three weeks.

When they arrived in St. Louis, a man at the train station, himself an Italian immigrant, heard them talking. He asked where they were heading. Angelo told him they were looking for a place to stay "in little Italy." He suggested they go see a priest named Father Capella at St. Ambrose Church in a section of town called The Hill.

Father Capella knew everyone on The Hill. He found Angelo and his family a place to stay right away. Not only that, he knew of a homebuilder, one of his parishioners, who was looking for bricklayers. Angelo went to the construction site the next morning and was hired on the spot.

The crew chief was impressed with Angelo from day one. He didn't know English. But he needed only glance at a blueprint to understand the scope of a project, and he had an intuitive sense for the flow of the work. He was strong and fast and took few breaks. Among the construction crews in town, all of them scrambling for good talent, Angelo quickly became a favorite.

Bricklaying was in his blood. His father and grandfather had also been bricklayers, and he hoped his own son would carry on the family tradition. And so when Dominic was only nine, Angelo began taking him to work on Saturdays.

Rose was not happy about this, but she had seen it coming for years. When Dominic was a toddler, Angelo would lie on the floor with him and show him how create little buildings with wooden blocks. By four, Dominic was not just constructing, but designing, his own little buildings. By five, he was creating little villages, sometimes sprawling from room to room in their small house. Rose grumbled about the mess. Angelo bought Dominic more blocks.

He took his son to work with him for the first time intending only that he watch. That was also his promise to Rose. But after watching his father butter the edges of a brick with wet cement, Dominic immediately picked up a trowel and joined him.

Angelo didn't say much. He didn't have to. The boy learned just by watching. And he worked alongside his father all day, laying one brick for every two of his father's, but just as straight.

Dominic was a natural. By ten, he had learned all the basics of bricklaying. By twelve, he was sketching interesting new designs for walkways and patios. Most bricklayers saw such surfaces as functional. Dominic saw them as art. He had a particularly keen sense for how the color and shape of a walkway or patio should fit with its natural surroundings.

"Brick is made from the earth," he would say to his father. "It should blend back in with the earth."

Dominic's designs were so good that Angelo shared them with his crew chief, who liked them so much that he began using them as a selling point with customers.

By fourteen, Dominic was as strong as his father and, by fifteen, he could handle small projects on his own. Angelo was thrilled.

In the early 1950s, homebuilding was booming in St. Louis. Builders vied for the best workers. Angelo always had work, and he earned more in a day than he would have in a week, or even a month, back home.

The family had been renting a place, but soon they had enough money to buy their own house. It was a small place, next to a bakery on The Hill. But it was theirs. And there was even enough money for Angelo to buy a used Chevy. He had never owned a car.

All three of them began to learn English. But Dominic picked it up much faster because only English was spoken in school at St. Ambrose. He fit in well there. Many of the other students were also the children of Italian immigrants. And they all lived on The Hill. The whole neighborhood had the feel of a big Italian family.

Life was good for the Carusos until Dominic was seventeen. Coming home from school one afternoon, he saw his father's car parked on the street. It was at least two hours before his father ever got home from work.

He went inside and heard a strange voice coming from his parents' bedroom. The door was open, and he looked in. It was Doctor DeToma. He was examining his mother, who was sitting up in bed. His father was sitting on a chair next to the bed. His mother's blouse was undone and, seeing Dominic, she quickly covered herself. He had never seen his mother in any state of undress.

His father got up and motioned to Dominic to come with him. He followed his father into the kitchen.

"What's going on, Dad?"

"Your mother is ill. The doctor says it is serious. He thinks it might be cancer."

His mother had always been frail, and lately she had not been feeling well. But cancer? It had never entered their minds.

But it ravaged her, and less than three months later, the day after Dominic's eighteenth birthday, it took her life.

Rose was Angelo's anchor and, without her, he felt adrift. He was not a man given to introspection. But now his world was rocked, and he began to reflect deeply on his situation.

And he realized that this place was not really his home, especially without Rose. His home was in Italy, the place he had known all his life, near the sea, among family and friends who spoke a language he did not labor to understand.

But he also realized that, for his son, this place was indeed now home. He knew Dominic would be successful here and carry on the family tradition. But he also knew that, as his son became a man, he himself would grow old, and he did not want to saddle his son with caring for an old man.

Moving to the U.S. was the toughest decision Angelo had ever made. But now he made one even tougher: to return to Italy. Fighting back tears, he told Dominic the day after he graduated from high school. Overwhelmed, Dominic said he would go too.

"No," his father said. "I want you to stay. You'll make a better life for yourself here."

A few days later, Angelo signed over the titles for his house and his car to his son. Then Dominic drove him to the train station and kissed him goodbye. That was in the summer of 1960.

He would never see his father again. And Peter Caruso, born a generation later, would never meet his grandfather.

...

"Sir, would you like something to drink?" the flight attendant asked.

She startled him.

"Yes, coffee, please. Black."

Sipping his coffee, Peter turned back to the window.

He thought again about that summer in the '80s, when he was fifteen years old and had worked with his father. He remembered the first day on the job and how odd it seemed to see him in work clothes. He usually left the house before Peter woke up. After work, he came in through the back door and went directly to his bathroom to take a shower. By the time Peter saw his father most evenings, for dinner, he had changed into dress clothes. That's how he dressed on the weekends too. On Sundays, he even wore a tie.

And it made him wonder: why was his father always so dressed up at home? So one day, he asked him.

"You see me now, Peter, as I usually am. But no one else does. They see the man I want them to see. That's the Dominic Caruso the world knows."

His father's answer puzzled him. And it begged the question: Why? Why did he want people to see him this way?

He didn't press his father that day. But over the course of the summer, he asked him many questions, and he learned so much.

He learned, for example, that when his father and grandfather were working on larger crews, the loud, rough men who framed the houses they bricked would call them "guineas." There was a pecking order in construction, and many of the workers looked down on bricklayers. "Only Italians" would do such menial work, they said.

His grandfather didn't seem very bothered by it, maybe because his English was not good. But it upset his father greatly.

It wasn't so much the name calling, but rather the idea that his work—and he, Dominic Caruso, by extension—was somehow less. At first, it made him angry. Then it made him wonder if he really did measure up.

At that point, in 1960, as much as he loved his work, given the option, he would have gladly done something else. Many of his friends were going off to college. He wished he could join them, then also do something respectable in the eyes of the world. But bricklaying was the only thing he knew and, now that he was alone, the only way he could make a living.

He couldn't change this. But he could change himself. He could change what people thought of him.

He began taking jobs he could do alone, so that few would ever see him at work in the first place. And when he was not working, he began wearing nice clothes. He sold his father's old Chevy and bought a new Buick. He began spending less time on The Hill and more time meeting new people, mainly young professionals, downtown. He sold the house on The Hill and got an apartment downtown.

Except for his work, he changed everything and became a new man.

...

Dominic was handsome, refined and spoke with a slight accent, which women found charming. One weekend, at a party, he met a beautiful first-grade teacher named Marisa. They were each sipping a glass of red wine. By the time their glasses were empty, they had fallen in love.

That evening, Marisa asked Dominic what he did for a living. When he told her, she was surprised, but not deterred. If anything, it made him even more intriguing.

But he was quick to insist that Marisa not talk about what he did for a living. He told her that, if anyone asked, she should simply say he "worked in design." She found this curious, but it was a half-truth she could live with.

In a year, they were married. They bought a small house in a suburb of St. Louis. Even with two incomes, they struggled to afford it, but no one would have guessed. They carried themselves with such grace.

And to everyone Peter knew growing up, his father was a simply a dashing, dapper, quiet man who always drove a new Buick.

"You become who people think you are, Peter," his father told him that summer, as his fifteen-year-old son worked beside him. "You become whoever you want to be."

...

"What do you want to do, Peter?" asked Mrs. Henry, his high school guidance counselor, three years later.

"I want to be a stock broker and live in New York."

"That's pretty specific," she said, smiling. "Why?"

"I want to make a lot of money."

"Do you know anything about becoming a stockbroker?"

"Not really. Just that I need to go to college."

"That's right. You'll need to major in business, probably finance. And you should think about an MBA too."

"Sounds good. What are my options?"

His confidence made her smile. She swiveled in her chair, slid open the top drawer of a metal file cabinet and picked out half a dozen brochures.

"Here are a few ideas to get you started. These are all good business schools. There are a few in the Midwest and few out East. The ones out East are a little pricey. You might want to start with the ones closer to home."

"Thank you," he said, grabbing the brochures and heading for the door.

"Peter."

"Yes?"

"Remember us when you get rich," she said, smiling.

"I will."

He went to his room after dinner that evening and read every brochure cover to cover. All the schools looked good. But he knew which one he wanted right away: NYU. It had a business school and was right in the heart of Manhattan. Tuition was steep. But he figured that between his father's modest income and his good grades, he would qualify for lots of aid and, he hoped, a scholarship or two.

And that's just what happened. And with the money he made interning at investment firms in Manhattan in the summers, he covered his housing costs and had spending money left over.

He earned his undergraduate degree in three years, then his MBA in a year, graduating with honors. He was heavily recruited and got offers from several top firms. They were all impressive. But Taft and Irving offered the best starting salary and a signing bonus. Plus he liked the way they called him "Mr. Caruso."

That was twenty years ago. He had indeed become a stock broker, made lots of money and was living in New York.

"You become whoever you want to be," his dad had told him. And so he had. But he still couldn't shake the feeling of being half-empty.

...

He called Maria as soon as his plane touched down.

"How's Dad?"

"Stable."

"Is he going to be okay?"

"We think so. They put in three stents. Oh, Pete. Dad had something the doctor called 'the widow-maker.' It was a close call."

"How's he feeling?"

"Pretty good. He's sitting up in bed. He's a strong man, Pete."

"How's mom?"

"She's okay."

"Good. We should be at the gate in a few minutes. I'll come straight to the hospital. Tell Mom and Dad I'll be there in about forty-five minutes."

"Okay, Pete. Room 405. See you soon."

...

It was early evening when he landed, but the sun had not yet set. He hadn't been home in nearly two years, and he was grateful for the chance to take in the landscape on the taxi ride before nightfall.

He had missed the low hills, the broad valleys, the rolling prairie. He remembered riding his bike along the back roads near his home as a boy and stopping in different places and pulling out his drawing book and sitting down to sketch a tree or a field or a stream.

It had filled him up. There was something about looking at a sunset or horses in a pasture or snow on a grove of pine trees and then expressing these things in his own way that made him happy.

And so he made hundreds of pictures: nature scenes, abstract designs, houses, barns, horses, cars and people, including portraits of his parents and his sister. He signed them all "Peter." He and his mother, who was his biggest fan, picked their favorites, and she framed them and hung them on his bedroom walls.

But when he became a teenager, his thoughts began to shift from the act of creating to the idea of painting for a living. Could he do it? Would he be good enough? Should he not strive for more? Would he make any money? What would people think of him?

No one had ever told Peter to become an artist. It just came naturally to him. But in high school, he began to have doubts. And for reasons he no longer remembered and maybe never fully understood, he put his pencils and paints away.

...

He found room 405, took a deep breath and peeked inside. His father was sitting up in bed, eating dinner. His mother and sister were sitting in chairs on either side of the bed.

"Oh!" the women cried and then rushed to him. He wrapped his arms around them, held them close and kissed them on the cheek.

"Peter, I'm so glad you're here," said his mother. She looked tired and so much older.

"We saw you on TV last week, Pete," said Maria. "You looked so good."

"But even more handsome in person," said his mother, pinching his cheek.

"Peter," said his father. "Thank you for coming."

He walked over to his father and shook his hand. He gripped Peter's hand tightly with his right, then clasped it with his left too. His hands were large and thick and calloused.

"It's good to see you, Dad. How are you?"

"Well, the doctor said I made it here just in time. And Father Earl said God doesn't need any more bricklayers in heaven today."

"I'm glad you're okay, Dad."

"So I guess I need to have a heart attack for you to come visit your mother."

"No, Dad. I'm sorry. I'll visit more often."

"We would love that, Peter," his mother said.

"We sure would," said Maria.

"How about this Christmas?" his mother asked, seizing the moment.

How could he say no?

"Yes, Mom. I'll come home this Christmas."

"Oh, Peter. That would mean so much to all of us."

"Amen," said Maria. "The kids would be so glad to see you again."

A nurse knocked and stepped into the room.

"May I take your tray, Mr. Caruso?"

"Absolutely," he said, pushing back his half-eaten dinner. "My compliments to the chef."

"Now, Dom," said his mother.

"Sorry," he said, grinning at Peter.

"You know," his mother said, "Maria and I were just talking about going down the cafeteria to get something to eat. Maybe this would be a good time for you two to catch up a bit."

"Maybe Peter's hungry too," his father said.

"No, I'm fine, Dad."

"Can we bring you something?" his mother asked.

"No, thanks."

"Okay. We'll be back soon. You boys be on your best behavior."

"We'll try, Mom. Enjoy your dinner."

His mother leaned down and gently kissed her husband on the lips.

"I love you, Dom."

"And I love you."

Peter pulled a chair over to the bed and sat down.

"Peter, there is something I need to tell you."

"What's that, Dad?"

"I was wrong."

"You were wrong?"

"Yes."

"About what?"

"I gave you some very bad advice. When we worked together that summer, I told you that you become who people think you are. But I was wrong."

"What do you mean, Dad?"

"You are who you are. What people think doesn't matter. The most important thing is to be yourself."

"I don't think you gave me bad advice, Dad."

"Yes, I did," he said, looking away. "And I set a bad example for you too. I'm a bricklayer. When I was young, I loved working with brick. To me, it was art. But over the years, I realized that most people don't see bricklaying that way. I wanted people to think I was something else, something more. I've lived my life as an imposter. And I regret that."

"Dad, I think you're being too hard on yourself."

"This is not just about me, Peter," looking his son in the eye. "It's about you too."

"About me?"

"Do you remember what you wanted to be when you were a boy?"

"Yeah. I wanted to be an artist."

"That's right. And do you remember what I told you about that?"

"No."

"I told you not to pursue it because there's no money in it. Become a stockbroker, I said. Move to New York. Those were my ideas, Peter, not yours. You were an artist. I put those foolish ideas in your head. It's the worst thing I've ever done."

"It's okay, Dad. I turned out all right, didn't I?"

His father looked at him and sighed.

"You're rich, Peter. But are you happy?"

He looked down and didn't answer. His mind was filled with the images of the pictures he had created as a boy, the pictures his mother had hung on the walls of his bedroom.

"We must be who we really are. It's the only way to be happy."

"Dad ..."

"I am a bricklayer, Peter. That's all I've ever been. And now I know that is enough."

Peter didn't know what to say.

"Find out who you are, Peter. It's not too late. And it will be enough."

He looked up at his father. His eyes were filled with tears. He had never seen his father cry.

"I'm sorry, Peter."

"It's okay, Dad."

He got up and held his father's left hand in both of his, then bent down and kissed him on the forehead.

"It's okay. All is forgiven."

...

He had driven his mother home in his father's Buick.

"You look good, but a little thin, Peter. Are you sure you're eating well?"

"I'm eating great, Mom."

"What did you have for dinner tonight?" He knew she knew the answer.

"Okay. I'll pick something up on the way."

"Don't be silly. I'll fix you some pasta when we get home."

"Mom, how are you doing?"

"I'm okay, thanks. Your father gave us quite a scare this morning. But he's going to be okay, and so I'm fine."

"You look tired, Mom. How's your health?"

"I'm fine, Peter. I'm just getting old. But I'm fine. Really."

"Good. Mom, Dad told me something back at the hospital I don't remember hearing before."

"Oh?"

"Yeah, he said he talked me out of becoming an artist when I was a kid. Is that true?"

His mother stiffened in her seat and looked straight ahead. She didn't answer.

"Mom?"

"Yes, it's true," she said quietly. Then she started to cry.

"I'm sorry, Mom. I didn't mean to upset you."

"It's okay, Peter," she said, dabbing her eyes with a tissue. "Your father just wanted the best for you. He wanted you to have the type of life he could only dream of."

"And how did you feel about that?"

"About what?"

"About me not becoming an artist?"

"It broke my heart."

"What?"

"It made me sad to see you stop painting. I should have put my foot down. But I hoped you would paint again one day. And then when you did so well in school and business, I started to think that your father was right."

"Do you really think he was right, Mom?"

"I'm proud of everything you've done, Peter."

"But do you think I missed my true calling?"

She didn't answer.

"Mom, you don't have to—"

"That's yours, Peter, something only you can know."

...

He parked in his parents' driveway. They had a garage. But he knew that, unless it was snowing, his father liked to park outside.

His mother unlocked the front door, and he followed her inside. The decor was spare, as it had always been. His parents had created a Feng shui look long before it was fashionable because it allowed them to buy less stuff.

"Make yourself at home, dear. You can sleep in your old room. Why don't you go change while I get supper ready?"

"Thanks, Mom. It's good to be home."

The house was small, a three-bedroom ranch, with no basement or upstairs. Peter's old bedroom was about the size of the kitchen in his apartment in New York.

He flipped on the light and looked around the room. Everything was just as it was when he was growing up.

On the walls, there must have been thirty paintings and drawings, each of them framed and signed "Peter." He had created all of them by the time he was twelve.

His old desk stood next to his bed. On it, in a frame, was a photograph of him in kindergarten, his first school picture. It was pasted on white paper, on which was printed "I am Peter Caruso" in crayon.

He pulled out the small wooden desk chair, sat down and picked up the frame.

"I am Peter Caruso," he said to himself.

Then he wondered aloud: "Who is Peter Caruso?"

He got up and changed into jeans and a sweatshirt. Then he sat down on his bed, grabbed his cell phone and dialed his boss' number, knowing he would no longer be in the office.

"Bill, it's Peter. I'm in St. Louis. My dad is going to be okay. But there are some things here that need my attention. I'm going to take a week. I'll call Pam and rearrange my schedule. Thanks for understanding, Bill. I'll see you in a week."

Peter got up and slid open his old closet door. His shirts and pants from high school still hung neatly inside. He looked up and spotted his old watercolor set still resting on a shelf.

He reached up and pulled down the white plastic case. He sat back down and placed the case on his desk. He snapped open the lid, revealing a row of eight oval cakes. The paint was dried and cracked, but the colors were still vibrant.

Peter plucked his old red paint brush out of a groove in the plastic and twisted the bristles between his fingertips. They were stiff. But he pushed them into the palm of his hand, and they gave way and became soft again, like new.

Forbidden Fruit

I don't remember how she looked. Of course, I was only four years old. Who remembers a face you saw at such a tender age, so long ago?

But I remember her name. It was Mary. She was my age. She lived two doors down on Culver Avenue. That's as far as my mother would let me wander.

I don't recall ever knocking on Mary's door to see if she could play because she was always outside. I guess she liked playing out there. I liked playing outside too. But most of my earliest memories are of being inside. Mary drew me out.

I had my own bedroom. It was at the end of the upper floor of our split-level home. It had a window. From there, I could see the house next door, beyond our white picket fence, and the backyard of the house beyond that. That was Mary's backyard.

In the morning, I would look out to see if she was there. When she was, I'd ask if I could go outside and play. I'd cut through our next-door neighbor's backyard and be with Mary once again.

I don't remember all the things we did together. In fact, I remember doing only one thing with Mary, and that was picking things off of plants in her yard and eating them.

We picked blackberries. We picked cherry tomatoes. We picked flowers. And we ate them. We didn't just stick our tongues out and give them a little lick. We put them in our mouths, chewed them up and swallowed them.

The berries tasted sweet, the tomatoes sour and the flowers spicy. I especially remember eating the flowers. They tasted liked they smelled, but there wasn't much to them. It was like eating an aroma.

I never would have thought of doing something like this or tried it on my own. But Mary seemed thrilled to be showing me around her yard and grazing this way. And she seemed happy that I was with her.

Somehow, my mother found out what we were doing. I suspect I told her. Either that or she saw blackberry stains around my mouth or maybe a flower petal stuck between my teeth. At any rate, she told me not to do it again.

"Those things could make you sick," she said.

Mary kept picking things and eating them, and I did too. Not that she told me to or even asked me to. But I had grown to like the taste of these wild things, and I loved being with Mary. I wanted to go where she went. I wanted to do what she did. When I spotted her through my bedroom window, I had to be with her.

We moved away just before I turned five. I remember seeing Mary out in her yard just before we left. I don't think I said goodbye, and I never saw her again.

I wonder if she kept picking wild things and eating them and, if she did, if she ever found anyone else to join her.

Mary was my first love. She drew me outside. She showed me a new world and gave me a taste of something exotic. She tempted me but let me choose. She made me happy.

Hold On

He drove a dark blue 1938 Buick Roadmaster. I wouldn't have known the year, the make or the model if my parents hadn't told me.

It was a relic. Whenever I saw it rolling down our street, I half expected gangsters to be hanging out of the windows, brandishing tommy guns. It didn't even sound like any other car on the road. All the cars I knew hummed or revved. This one clicked, like an egg timer.

But its driver seemed even more ancient and mysterious. We knew him only as Old Man Hopkins. None of us had ever met him. Even our parents called him Old Man Hopkins.

He lived at the end of our street in a house that was much older than all the others in our neighborhood. Once in a while, I would see him driving past my house. Maybe it was those small car windows. But I never got a good look at him. This, of course, only added to the mystery.

...

In the summer of 1970, when I was twelve, I decided to make as much money as I could by cutting grass, and I went door to door looking for customers.

Old Man Hopkins' yard was huge, and it was a mess. So one morning, I psyched myself up, rode my bike down to the end of our street, walked up his long gravel driveway, climbed the steps to his front porch, took a deep breath and knocked on his door.

The front door opened. I could barely see him through the outer screen door. He looked smaller and even older than I expected.

"Yes?"

"Mr. Hopkins?"

"Yes?"

"My name is Bill. I live down the street. I was wondering if you might need someone to cut your grass."

"Do you mean you?"

"Yes."

"How much do you charge?"

"Three dollars."

"I have a pretty big yard."

"That's okay. I can handle it."

"I'll give you five. When can you cut it?"

"This afternoon," I stammered.

"Deal. I'll be here. Come see me when you're done."

I had never cut a yard so big. It took three hours and two tanks of gas. When I was finished, I knocked on the old man's front door. He stepped out on the porch and looked around.

"Nice job," he smiled.

"Thanks."

"I think you've earned a little more than five dollars today," he said, handing me a ten. "That should cover your gas too."

"Thank you!"

"You're welcome. You thirsty?"

"Yeah."

"Hang on. I'll be right back."

In a minute, he came back out with a cold, eight-ounce bottle of Coke.

"Here you go."

"Thanks."

I chugged it.

"Can you cut my grass again next week?"

"Sure. What day is best?"

"Whatever works for you. I'm here all the time. Just knock when you're done, and we'll settle up."

"Sounds great. Thanks again, Mr. Hopkins," I said, making my way down his steps.

"See you next week, Bill."

I ended up cutting Mr. Hopkins' grass every Wednesday morning that summer. Nobody could believe it. I could hardly believe it myself. And what was even more incredible was that each time, when I was finished, Mr. Hopkins had lunch waiting for us on his front porch.

"I suspect I'm a bit of a mystery around here," he said the first time we sat down for lunch.

"Yeah, you might say that."

"Well, I understand," he grinned. "What would you like to know about me, Bill?"

His question caught me by surprise.

"How long have you had that car?"

It was a stupid question but the first thing that popped into my head.

"I bought it new in 1938. Would you like to see it?"

"Yeah."

After lunch, we walked the gravel path to a one-car garage behind his house. He struggled to lift the door, so I helped him push it up.

And there it was, like some rare antiquity on display in a museum.

"It looks so old," I blurted out.

"It is. But it still runs well."

"Is that why you've kept it?"

"No."

"Why then?"

He told me he bought it when his son, his only child, was a boy and that he used to take his wife and son for long drives in the country on Sundays.

Then he told me that his son was killed during the war and that he lost his wife to cancer less than a year later. He had been living alone in that house ever since.

"I keep this car because it's my only link with the two people I've loved most in this world," he told me. "You hold on to what means the most."

"I'm sorry for your loss," I said.

"Thank you, Bill. Would you like to go for a ride?"

"Sure."

And that's the way it went every Wednesday that summer. I would cut Mr. Hopkins' grass, he would serve us lunch and we would go for a ride in his Roadmaster.

When my friends found out, they wanted a ride too. Who wouldn't want to ride in that car? I asked Mr. Hopkins. He said yes.

And so every Wednesday afternoon, my friends would pile into the back seat, and Mr. Hopkins, who seemed lit up by our oohs and ahs, would take us all for a ride. I always got to sit in the front.

...

That winter, Mr. Hopkins died. In his will, he stipulated that all his assets be sold and the proceeds given to charity.

Except one thing: his car. He gave that to me.

I keep it in my garage. I don't drive it much, but it still runs well. And with my kids and their friends, it's legendary.

You hold on to what means the most.

Free

Henry Wilson finished his book, stood up and shuffled over to the bookshelves which took up more than half the wall of his library. He carefully slid the book back in its place, then stepped over to the window. It was dusk. A light snow was falling. Christmas lights bordered the windows of the building across the street. "Silent Night" wafted up from a shop below.

Christmastime always made Henry think of his father. He remembered walking with him on the sidewalks near their apartment on the Lower East Side when he was a boy. It was a Christmas Eve tradition. His father stuffed a roll of singles into Henry's coat pocket. When they would come across someone who looked down on his luck, his father would nod, and Henry would reach into his pocket, pull out a dollar bill and hand it to the person, wishing him a Merry Christmas.

Henry's father was a man of modest means. It took him all year to save those dollar bills. But giving them away fit with his philosophy. He had brought it with him from Ireland.

"Strive to give away all you own," he would often tell his young son, "lest it own you."

Henry greatly admired his father. But he put aside his advice. When he graduated from college, he went to work for a big accounting firm and began to make good money. He rented a nice apartment in Midtown Manhattan.

Henry never married, and he lived frugally. He took part of his paycheck every week and gave it to a colleague to invest. Early in his career, the stock market was up and down. He was tempted to shift his money to a savings account, which seemed safer. But his colleague counseled patience, and Henry agreed to stay the course.

It was the right choice. By the time he retired, his portfolio was worth more than two million dollars.

Every so often, Henry considered giving some of it away. But he knew that, if he lived long enough, he would either need home care or be forced to move into a retirement center. Both options were expensive. He might need every penny.

He also still worried about the market. A downturn could put a serious dent in his portfolio. Over time, he grew so concerned about the risk that he moved all his holdings into accounts with four different banks near his apartment. He liked the idea of keeping his money.

He had lived in that same apartment for more than sixty years. When he moved in, the monthly rent was fifty dollars. Now it was approaching four thousand.

Sometimes, Henry felt trapped by his luxurious surroundings. He considered moving. But there were no inexpensive places in Manhattan any more.

He often thought about the tiny, cramped apartment where he'd grown up. He had nightmares about losing his money and having to live in a place like that again.

So he hung on to his money and his apartment too.

...

At Christmastime, Henry always walked to Rockefeller Center to see the big tree. Now, though, in his mid eighties, he decided to take a taxi. He had the driver take him to 5th Avenue and park there so he could gaze across the plaza at the spectacular tree.

He remembered his parents taking him to see it when he was a boy. His father told him he worked on a construction crew there during the Depression. The workmen decided to pool their money and buy a sparse, twenty-foot balsam fir. They put it up in the mud and decorated it with handmade ornaments from their homes. It was the very first Rockefeller Christmas tree.

Henry wished his father and all the men on his crew were there to see the majestic tree their generous efforts had birthed all those years ago.

He was about to roll up his window when a man approached his taxi. His clothes were ragged. He had a grey, wiry beard. He leaned against the left, rear door of the taxi, pressing the palms of his hands on the chrome frame of the open window.

"Hey!" yelled the driver, looking in his side mirror and rolling his window down. "Get outta here!"

Henry's instinct was to roll up his window. But the man's fingers were now gripping the upholstery of the inside of the door.

Henry looked into his face. His eyes were sad.

"Mister, can you spare a dollar?" he asked.

Henry wasn't sure what to do. Then the driver opened his door and stepped out onto the sidewalk.

"I said get outta here!" Henry heard him shout.

Then he saw the beggar being yanked backwards. His hands grabbed wildly at the air as he tried in vain to maintain his footing. He fell to the ground.

The driver got back in, slammed his door and rolled his window back up.

Henry looked out at the man, who was struggling to get up and looking toward his still-open window.

"Sorry about that, sir," said the driver, throwing his taxi into gear and speeding away.

...

The next morning, after breakfast, Henry called a former colleague to ask how much money he would need if he moved away and lived another five years. His former colleague gave him a number.

Henry got dressed in his only remaining business suit. He pulled a suitcase from the back of his closet, went downstairs and hailed a taxi.

He had the driver let him out at the first of his four banks. There he asked to withdraw all his money, in cash, and close his account.

At first, the manager tried to talk him out of it, no doubt wondering if the old man had lost his mind. But he could see Henry was perfectly coherent, and he abided, even arranging the tightly bundled stacks of hundred dollar bills in Henry's suitcase.

Henry took a taxi back to his apartment and lugged his suitcase inside. He lay it on his bed and transferred the money into one of his dresser drawers.

Then he grabbed his suitcase, went back downstairs and again hailed a taxi. This time, he took it to his second bank and repeated the exercise. Then, after taking the money back to his apartment, he went to his third bank and did the same thing.

That afternoon, having withdrawn most of his savings, Henry changed into old clothes, put on an overcoat and a wool cap, reached into his dresser drawer and stuffed his pockets full of hundreds.

Over the next four days, Henry made more than twenty trips to poor neighborhoods in the Bronx, Brooklyn, Harlem and Queens. He walked up and down the sidewalks, looking for people who looked down on their luck.

"Merry Christmas," he said to each of them, handing each a crisp bill.

He might have created a frenzy. But each person he approached was stunned and simply said thank you. Besides, who would suspect an old man of handing over his fortune to strangers?

With each taxi ride back to his apartment for more money, Henry felt more free and at peace. He went back and forth, venturing out heavy and returning home light, until just before midnight on Christmas Eve, when his pockets were, at last, empty.

The Clearing

He stopped walking, then turned around, full circle, searching the trees in the fast-fading light for a clearing or a way out. But there was no clearing, no trail, no end to the woods. And with darkness falling fast, he began to realize that soon he would be able to see nothing at all.

His name was David, and he was twelve years old. He had explored these woods countless times, but almost always with his older brother, Charles, or friends. And he had never ventured this far.

...

School had let out early that afternoon, and Charles wouldn't be home until after football practice. His parents would be late. Once again, David and Charles would make their own dinner, usually macaroni and cheese or some frozen meal popped in the microwave, and watch ESPN as they ate, barely exchanging a word. Sometimes Charles would take his food up to his room. David could hardly remember the last time they had had dinner together as a family.

With a few hours to kill, he sat at the kitchen table, eating a bowl of Frosted Flakes, staring out the back window.

He thought about texting a friend, maybe getting together to play video games. But then he dismissed the idea because he knew that would mean riding his bike nearly two miles, mainly on rough roads. He knew he could handle it. The problem would be on the way home. It would be getting dark, and his father had forbidden him from riding his bike that late in the day.

And he couldn't invite anyone over because none of his friends' moms would let their sons visit without an adult at home. All these moms had two things in common: they all had twelve-year-old boys; and they were all, therefore, suspicious of twelve-year-old boys.

More and more, David found himself alone. He could find ways to fill the time, but not the space. He felt empty. And his emptiness was caused not by an absence of things, but of affection.

Now, in the early afternoon, he sat alone in his kitchen and watched big, grey clouds move in. The temperature was in the low 40s, warm for Maine in early December. But there was a chill in the air, and the wind was kicking up. It blew through the tall trees at the edge of the woods that bordered his back yard, and the sun, already low in the sky, cast shadows across the faded red and yellow leaves which covered all but small patches of pale-green grass.

He was learning to live in solitude. But there is a fine line between solitude and loneliness, and today he was feeling lonely. As David listened to the wind and watched the trees sway and the shadows dance and thought about the prospect of another afternoon alone, he felt drawn to the comfort and the company of the woods.

The woods were always there for him. When he was very young, his father used to take him and Charles for hikes. His mother packed their lunch in a big brown bag: peanut butter and jelly sandwiches, apples and cookies. His father carried the bag and a thermos of chocolate milk in a small knapsack. They would stop along the trail when they found a stump grand enough to serve as a table. And they would sit together on a log, eating, taking turns drinking chocolate milk from the red cap of the thermos and reveling in their manly adventure.

As the years went by, though, the three of them took fewer hikes together. His father always seemed to have something else to do— work, some project, going out with his friends, even taking a nap. By the time David was eight, the boys stopped asking him to go.

But David and Charles had kept hiking. Not only that, they kept going deeper into the woods.

One day, they hiked all the way through the woods to a river. They stumbled upon it together. They had just made their way through a thick stand of trees. Suddenly, before them lay a meadow of tall grasses and wildflowers sloping down to a river. Cypress trees lined its banks. It looked like paradise. And knowing he had discovered it with his big brother made David feel special, like he had helped find a treasure which only the two of them shared.

After that, they would hike to the river often. Sometimes, they would bring their fishing poles. Charles taught him how to set his line and fish. Sometimes, in the summer, they would spend an entire day there.

Sometimes, David would bring a friend or two along. They would always follow the same trail, which became so familiar to him. But to his friends, everything was new. He loved watching them experience it all for the first time. He loved watching his brother lead the way. And he especially loved when they got to the "reveal" of the river. Seeing it for the first time, his friends would always be astonished, and David would look up at Charles, who would be smiling. He looked like a king, and David felt like a prince.

These were his favorite memories. And even though they were distant memories now, and even though Charles no longer went hiking with him, the woods continued to give him comfort. In a way, they had become his best friend. And so now, on that blustery afternoon, he decided to go for a hike.

...

He zipped up his coat and pulled down a red wool cap over his short brown hair. He eyed his gloves but decided against them. If it got cold, he could keep his hands in his pockets.

He pulled the back door tight and kicked a path through the thick layer of leaves and twigs across the lawn. At the edge of his yard, a dirt trail led into the woods. It was damp from a light rain the day before, but not muddy. That was good because he was wearing his new Chuck Taylors, and if they got muddy, his mother would be mad.

With the sun so low, the woods were darker than he expected. For a moment, he thought about returning to the house to get his pocket flashlight, the one he used to read in bed at night. But he would be home before dark, and so he decided to keep going.

He stepped into the woods. The air was heavy with the scent of wet leaves, and the trail felt cold under his feet. He hadn't been there since the hardwood trees had gone bare. Everything looked so sparse now. But this was good because it meant he could see farther. He would need that advantage because the sky was now overcast and, even without their leaves, the trees shrouded the dying light.

It was more than a woods, really. It was an old-growth forest, filled with an astonishing array of trees: aspen, birch, red and sugar maples, oaks, white and red pines, balsam fir and spruces. His father said they had moved there, before David was born, to be near "a wild place." And this was a wild place. He had seen many deer in these woods. Once he had seen a red fox. Charles told him there were even mountain lions.

The prospect of wild animals might have given him pause about venturing into the woods alone, especially so late in the day. Once, he would have found it too scary. But his life had become too routine, too predictable, too safe. And now it was the mystery, precisely the not knowing, that drew him in.

And he was glad to get out of the house. For him, it had become such a cold and empty place. He knew Charles would come home and barely acknowledge him. He had been this way for more than a year, since he started high school. These days, Charles ignored just about everyone. All he cared about was sports and going online. He spent hours on his iPad in his bedroom. Their mother would sometimes scold him for spending too much time on his computer and not enough time on his homework. She used to try to impose "computer time." But it never worked. And she wasn't around enough anymore to even know when he was online anyway.

...

Now David came to a split in the trail. He had been there many times. But he had always gone to the right, never to the left.

To the right, the trail went on for another mile or so and led to the river.

To the left, the trail stretched for several miles. His brother had told him it led to a clearing and "civilization," although he had never actually gotten that far himself. He had walked part of it. But he found it very tough, with lots of hills, heavy brush and deep creeks. And so they never took that trail, and Charles warned him against ever trying it.

But one day, as they came to the divide and having grown so comfortable in the woods, David asked if they could take the longer trail.

"No," Charles said flatly.

"Why not?" David asked. "You know we could do it."

"I don't know that," his brother replied. "Besides, we're not sure where it goes."

"But you said it leads to a clearing."

"That's only what I've heard. I've never been there. And even if it's true, it's way too far for you."

"Okay," David said, "Then I'll go there by myself."

Charles stopped and turned around.

"Don't even think about it," he said. "You'd get lost. You'd never make it."

For the moment, David backed off. But that longer and more dangerous trail continued to intrigue him, and he never forgot the prohibition, which seemed to him a dare.

Now he stood at the divide and thought about Charles, the person he had idolized growing up, the person who used to show him the way and protect him, the person who no longer wanted anything to do with him.

He stood at the divide, contemplating all these things, and stepped to his left.

...

David thought about his parents too. They were seldom together these days. They left for work and got home at different times. They ate their meals separately. They slept in separate bedrooms. And when they were together, they argued bitterly. He didn't know which was worse: the silent tension or the fighting.

It hadn't always been this way. He remembered his father kissing his mother on the cheek when he got home from work. He remembered them sitting on the couch together. He remembered them laughing together, talking together.

Sadly, those were distant memories now. These days, his parents barely spoke to one another. They no longer even called each other by name. He wasn't sure why they had drifted apart. But he knew exactly when they began to fight.

It was one of his earliest memories. He was five. His father had taken him to a department store. They were in the toy aisle. David was drawn to a red, plastic truck with big, knobby tires. He reached up on his tiptoes and took it off the shelf. It was so heavy that he had to use both hands. He set the truck down on the linoleum floor, rolled it back and forth and pushed it down the aisle as hard as he could. The rubber tires made a whirring sound. The truck hit the bottom of a metal shelf, hard, and bounced off, without overturning. Cool!

"Hey, Dad!" he said. "Can we buy this?"

But there was no answer. He looked up. His father was not there. He walked to the end of the aisle, but his father was not there either. He felt a pain in his stomach. He dropped the red truck.

He ran to the next aisle and peered down it. He saw strangers, but not his father.

"Daddy!" he called, now running past every aisle. But there was still no answer.

"Daddy!" he screamed. Then he stopped. He was afraid and out of breath, and he started to cry.

The whole thing was like a bad dream and, as with all dreams, the details had faded over time. He could no longer remember exactly how he got to the customer service desk. He could only remember telling the lady there that his name was David, then hearing "Would the father of a little boy named David please come to the customer service desk?" on the loudspeaker.

Then he saw his father running towards him, his arms flapping at his sides. At first, David almost didn't recognize him. His eyes were wild, and his normally stoic face looked pained and distorted. But then his father saw him, sitting on the counter, and his face changed. It looked like it was melting. Tears ran down his cheeks. And as his father approached him, he called him by name and, for the first time David could remember, he grabbed him and held him close.

They talked in the car on the way home. How did it happen? They figured that his father had stepped away for only a moment, while David was playing with the toy truck. And when they couldn't find each other, they headed in opposite directions. So the more they searched, the more they got separated.

It seemed to make so much sense in the car. But it all fell apart when they got home. His mother blew up.

"How could you be so stupid?" she screamed at his father.

He had no defense. But by then, his father had begun to regain his composure. And rather than take it, he gave it right back. David no longer remembered what either of his parents said that day. He just remembered them yelling at each other into the night.

And he remembered how, after that, nothing ever seemed the same again. His parents became cold and distant, initially toward each other and eventually toward the boys too. His family seemed to break apart, a "family" only in that they were all still living in the same house.

If only he had left that truck on the shelf, if only he had only stayed with his father, if only he had not upset his mother, none of this would have happened.

...

David had been walking for well over an hour now. His brother had been right: this trail was a lot tougher. In fact, it was exactly as he had described it.

A tree trunk had fallen across the first creek he came to. The water was at least five feet below. But the tree trunk was wide and sturdy, and David was able to cross it without a problem, even looking down at the water rushing by.

Soon he came to a second creek. A fallen tree stretched across it too. But it was much thinner, and the creek was probably ten feet below. He stepped onto it and felt dizzy. So he climbed down and made his way to the narrowest part of the creek and decided to cross there.

Four rocks formed a jagged line through the water. The middle two were nearly submerged. None of the rocks was big enough for both of his feet, so he had to balance himself, one foot on one rock at a time. He got halfway across. His right foot was on the second rock, his left on the third. Only one more rock to go. But his left foot slipped, tipping him off balance, and he fell into the stream, landing on his hands and knees.

The stream was shallow, but he was soaked from his thighs down and from his hands to his elbows. The water was so cold it stung his skin. He jumped to his feet and sloshed through a ripple of water to the shore. There, he faced a steep bank. There was no way around it, only up. So he grabbed onto small trees and roots in the earthen hillside to pull himself up to where the land became flat again.

He stood there, shaken up by his fall and now beginning to tremble from being cold and wet. Between the heavy brush and the fading light, the trail was now nearly impossible to see. He drew a deep breath and tried to collect his thoughts. He guessed he was now easily more than halfway to the end of the trail. Maybe he could make it to the clearing Charles had told him about. For sure, if he turned back now, he would never make it home before dark. He decided to go on.

...

Just a week before, his mother had picked him up after school to go shopping. He was not used to seeing her so early in the day. But she had gotten off work early and needed to do some Christmas shopping. So she texted him and told him to meet her as school was letting out.

They drove to Rike's. It was a sprawling, ancient department store, known for its elaborate Christmas displays, including Christmas trees set up along the awnings over the main entrances to the building, which took up a whole city block. Some people drove hundreds of miles to shop there at Christmas. Some came just to see it.

Holly, tinsel and fake snow adorned every aisle. Christmas music and the smell of popcorn filled the air. And of course, Santa was there, enthusiastically receiving a steady stream of happy and frightened children.

David remembered his parents bringing him and Charles there years ago to see Santa. Now, his mother walked right past the big man, seeming not to notice.

"You need new tennis shoes," she said in a voice decidedly out of tune with the warm music. "Come on."

Then she made a beeline for the kids department. His mother always walked fast when she shopped. He had to quicken his pace to keep up.

In the boys' shoes section, there were lots of great options. But he knew what he wanted: Chuck Taylors. Red ones.

"Are you sure?" his mother asked. "And red?"

"Yes, Mother," he said.

"Okay. I guess you know what you want."

He asked the clerk if he could wear them home.

"Absolutely," she said, smiling and putting his old shoes in the box. "Of course, you know, you'll now be the coolest young man in the store."

"Thanks," he said, smiling.

He stood up and began to walk around. He loved the feel of new tennis shoes. But just then his mother, who seemed to be in a hurry, said, "Let's go."

He wasn't sure where they were going, but he followed his mother closely as they made their way through the crowded store. Then he remembered: Rike's had an old-fashioned soda fountain. It was in the corner of the store, right where they were heading!

David and Charles used to like to sit at the counter and watch the "soda jerk" make milkshakes. He remembered when his parents used to have to lift him up onto one of the tall, red vinyl, swivel bar stools. Now, he grabbed the edge of the counter and hoisted himself up. It was still a bit of a climb.

He expected his mother to sit down beside him. But instead, she took a twenty-dollar bill out of her purse and laid it on the counter.

"Order yourself something to eat and drink," she said. "I'm going to do some shopping."

"When will you be back?" he asked.

"I don't know," she said impatiently. "I've got a few things to buy, so I shouldn't be gone too long. If you need me, text me."

Then, looking him in the eye, she added: "And don't go anywhere."

He ordered a hamburger and French fries and, of course, a chocolate malt. At first, it felt cool to be on his own. But then he noticed that most of the others at the lunch counter were children with their parents. He was the only one there by himself.

When he was finished eating, he swiveled around on his stool and watched children holding their parents' hands, moving from one department, one display, one toy to the next. He longed to be a part of it. But he knew this was no longer his life. And he felt so alone.

He kept an eye on his phone for a text from his mother. But no text ever came. Finally, after two hours, she returned, with shopping bags hanging like candy canes from her arms.

She still seemed to be in a hurry and simply said, "Let's go."

...

Now David looked down at his new shoes. They were covered with mud. So were his jeans. His mother would be mad.

But when wasn't she mad these days?

More and more, her anger seemed to be directed at David. Maybe it was because his father and his brother weren't around much, making him an easy target.

All he knew was that everything he did seemed to set her off anymore. His music was too loud. His grades were too low. His clothes didn't match. His room was a mess. He didn't speak up.

His friends got in trouble for these things too. Maybe he was too sensitive, he thought. Maybe his mother didn't mean to hurt him. Maybe it was not about him at all. Maybe his mother was searching for a clearing too.

David did not plan to follow that trail so deep into the woods that day or be so far from home. But he knew that, by leaving, he would no longer be a nuisance. And he was tired of being a nuisance.

So he left. He just left.

...

The sun was almost down now, and the thick clouds blocked any light from the moon and the stars. David had lost the trail. In the dim light, he could make out only the silhouette of the trees all around him. The trees were like a fortress now. They made him feel safe.

But he was also cold and tired. He had walked a long way. He must be near the clearing. If only he could find it.

But then he remembered Charles had said he wasn't even sure there was a clearing. Maybe he'd made it up.

It reminded him of being lost in that store, more than half a lifetime ago. Except now, he knew he was on his own, and he understood how it felt to be truly alone.

He needed to rest. And so he stopped walking and stood still. He was surrounded by a small grove of trees. He crouched and felt along the ground for dry leaves, which he gathered into a little pile.

He lay down on the bed of leaves. He pulled his hat down over his ears and eyes, stuffed his hands into the pockets of his coat, drew his knees up to his chest and curled up, as tightly as he could.

He knew there were owls and coyotes in the woods at night. But tonight, everything was quiet. Everything was peaceful. And he was happy because, for so long now, all he had wanted was some peace.

He felt a gust of wind and heard the rustling of the last leaves on branches high above, the leaves which, despite the change of seasons, refused to let go. There are some leaves on some trees whose connection remains strong, no matter how fierce the winter. There is something inside, unseen, which binds them.

Then he heard a voice in the distance, a woman's voice.

"David!"

Then a man's voice.

"David!"

Then he heard them calling his name together.

They were the voices of his parents. It had been so long since he had heard them in unison. The very idea made him glad.

David stood up and pulled his cap back from over his eyes. Through the darkness, he could now see a clearing. Reaching out to the trees to guide him, he began walking toward the voices and shouted, "I am here!"

Unplugged

The early morning sun shot through the cracks in the blinds on her bedroom window and jolted her awake.

For a moment, the girl struggled to get her bearings. Then she realized her alarm hadn't gone off. She reached for her phone. It was dead. WTF!

"Mom!" she cried.

No answer.

"Mom! Why didn't you wake me up?!"

Still no answer.

"Mom!"

"We're downstairs, honey!"

Crap! Now she was going to be late for school. She threw off her covers, slipped on her flannel PJ bottoms, stalked down the hallway and stomped down the stairs.

Her parents were sitting in the family room, staring at the TV.

"What's going on?" she asked.

Her dad held up one hand.

"Hang on," he said. "Just watch."

On TV, she saw people gathering in the street and police in riot gear.

"Where is that?" she asked.

"New York," her dad replied.

"What's happening?"

"The internet's down, honey," her mom said.

"What?"

"All over the world," her dad added.

"WTF!"

"Excuse me, young lady?" her mom said.

"Sorry. You mean the internet's down everywhere?"

"Yeah," her dad said. "It crashed overnight."

"How?"

"Nobody knows," said her mom. "Probably a virus. Or maybe a cyberattack."

"Whatever it was," said her dad, "we've never seen anything like it."

On TV, crowds were gathering outside of banks in London. People were shouting, trying to push their way into the banks. The police had formed a line and were trying to hold the crowds back.

"What are those people doing?" the girl asked.

"They're trying to get their money," her dad said.

"Why can't they get their money?"

"Everything's offline," her mom said. "Businesses, the government, schools, even hospitals."

"This is going to get ugly," her dad said.

And as they sat there watching TV, things began to get ugly before their eyes. The crowds, now thousands strong in some cities, began to overwhelm the police and break through barricades. Clouds of tear gas made it hard to see exactly what was happening. But the sound of glass shattering signaled the banks were not safe.

"All hell's breaking loose," her dad said.

"People are afraid," her mom said.

Then her dad got up, stepped over to the hall closet and slipped on a pair of old loafers he kept there.

"Where are you going?" her mother asked anxiously.

"I'm going down to the bank," he said.

"But it's closed," she said.

"You don't know that."

"It's closed, Bob," she said. "Everything is closed."

He knew she was right. He kicked his shoes into the closet, walked slowly back into the family room and sat down on the sofa next to his wife. They both stared blankly at the TV. They looked so lost. The girl had never seen her parents this way.

Then she caught a glimpse of a picture on the mantle. It was a photo of the three of them standing on the shore of Lake Michigan, the sun rising behind them. She was nestled between her parents, her little arms holding them tight. She looked so small, and they all looked so happy.

It had been her favorite vacation. She remembered the three of them eating breakfast in the kitchen of the musty, wooden house they rented on the lake. They spent so little time together anymore.

Then she stood up, grabbed the remote and turned off the TV.

"Hey!" her dad yelled. "Why'd you do that?"

"Let's have breakfast," she said.

"What?" he replied, looking puzzled.

"Yes," her mom joined in. "I'll make pancakes."

The girl looked at her dad and smiled.

"Daddy, let's have breakfast."

He looked at his daughter. Suddenly, she looked so tall.

"Okay," he said, standing up.

The three of them went into the kitchen, where they ate together, unplugged and reconnected.

The Pin Insulator

As soon as his aunt lay down for her afternoon nap, the boy took off on his bike. He sliced through his subdivision, then made his way through the narrower streets of the older neighborhoods, where his mother had grown up. Her father had grown up on one of the farms just beyond.

He had heard there is a river beyond the farmland. He had always wanted to see it. But his mother would never let him go that far, not even with friends. Now, though, his parents were gone. They were attending his grandfather's funeral, and his aunt, who was in charge for a few days, liked to take very long naps.

The boy came to a cornfield at the edge of the older neighborhood. He laid his bike down there and walked between the rows of corn toward where he had heard the river would be.

At the other end of the cornfield lay a meadow filled with tall grasses, milkweed and wildflowers. In the distance, he could see a thicket of oak trees. Off to the right stood a red barn and a white farm house.

Something shiny caught his eye. Curious, he made his way through the heavy grass to check out whatever was glistening in the afternoon sun.

Whatever it was, it was attached to the top of a fallen telephone pole whose end was jutting up through the tall grass. As he got closer, he realized the pole was resting on another one on the ground and that there was a whole line of fallen telephone poles that stretched across the meadow, obscured by the grass.

Now he could see what was glistening. It was a fist-sized, aqua-colored, grooved, cylindrical glass object, rounded at the end. It was sitting on a wooden pin which extended from the cross arm of the telephone pole. Looking more closely, he could see that the inside of the glass was threaded, and he decided to try to unscrew it.

But as soon as he touched it, a current shot though his body and knocked him backwards. For a few moments, he could see nothing but a white light. Then everything around him was clear again.

Except that now the telephone poles were all standing, with wires stretching between them. Glass objects, just like the one he had seen, dotted the cross arms of every pole.

The boy thought he was seeing things. Then he heard the splash of water. It was coming from beyond the trees up ahead. It must be the river, he thought.

As he headed toward the trees, he heard someone singing. It sounded like the voice of a boy.

He walked through the trees. There was the river. Not far from the bank stood a boy in water up to his waist.

"Hey!" he yelled up.

"Hey!"

"Do you want to go swimming? The water's warm today."

"I didn't bring my trunks."

"Trunks? Who needs trunks? I swim naked. Actually, I can't swim. But I don't go out very far. Do you know how to swim?"

"Yeah."

"Then lose your clothes and take a dip. It feels great!"

Being a boy, whose parents were out of town, he took off his clothes and waded in.

"What's your name?" he said to the boy in the water.

"Henry. What's yours?"

"John."

"Watch yourself, John. The rocks are slippery, and the bottom drops off in a hurry."

"Do you live around here, Henry?"

"Yeah. My family lives on the farm just beyond those trees."

"Can I ask you something about those telephone poles over there?"

"Shoot."

"Have they always been standing up like that?"

"What do you mean?"

"Just a little while ago, I could have sworn they were all down on the ground."

"What are you talking about? That's how we get our electricity out here."

Just then Henry disappeared under the water. When he bobbed back up, his arms flailing, he cried, "Help!"

From the panicked look on his face, John knew he wasn't joking.

"Hang on!" he cried, diving in.

John was a strong swimmer. He grabbed Henry around the chest and side stroked towards shore. Soon, they were back in shallow water, standing up.

"That was close," John said.

"Too close," Henry coughed. "Thanks for saving me."

"No problem."

Henry lay down on the grassy bank, still catching his breath.

"Now what were you saying about those telephone poles?"

"Oh, nothing. I took a fall back there. I think I might have been seeing things."

"Well, those poles better be standing. We depend on them for electric and telephone. Plus, I like climbing them. Well, I've got to get home," he said, pulling on his undershirt. It was the old sleeveless, tank top kind.

"Me too," John said, stepping into his jeans. "It's good to meet you, Henry. I'm glad you're okay."

"Good to meet you too, John. Thanks for being here today."

John's parents got home the next morning. They brought back some of his grandfather's things, including a bunch of old photographs. His mother spread them out on the dining room table.

John was astonished to see a glass object just like the one he had seen yesterday.

"What's that?" he asked.

"That's a pin insulator."

"A what?"

"A pin insulator. They used to use them on telephone poles to keep the wires in place."

"Where'd you get it?"

"It was grandpa's. He loved telling us how he climbed up a telephone pole as a boy and crawled out on the crossbeam to get it. He used it as a paperweight for years. I thought you might like to have it."

John went over to the table and picked it up. It was heavy and felt thick in his hands. Then he looked down at the photographs.
"Who's this?" he asked.
"That's grandpa, probably when he was about your age."
John gasped. It was Henry.

The Test

On a mutual dare, Brad, David and Jason, all nineteen and the best of friends, decided to take a year off of college and spend it together, camping in the woods of the Adirondack Mountains.

They set up camp in a primitive site about a mile from a lake. Each of them pitched his own tent and built a lean-to next it. They packed in as much dried food as they could carry and went into town once a month to replenish their supplies. They caught trout, bass and perch in the lake and cooked it for dinner nearly every night.

Fishing from shore was easy. But when the weather turned cold in the fall and the lake began to freeze, fishing became a challenge.

None of them had ever ice fished. It took them time to learn how to use a gas-powered augur to drill holes in the ice and set tip-ups.

They made a rule that when one of them was ice fishing, the other two needed to be nearby, just in case the ice should crack. This usually meant two of them were sitting around a small fire at the edge of the lake, staying warm, while one sat on a bucket on the ice, shivering and praying for the flag to go up.

At night, they sat around the fire, talking. They'd grown up together. But now they'd been away from each other, at colleges, for nearly a year. It was good to catch up.

But in sharing their latest experiences, they also began to realize they were changing. They'd always gotten along so well. But now they began to argue and bicker.

By winter, there were whole days when they didn't speak to one another. They simply stayed in their tents. The cold became an alibi for not engaging.

...

By early March, the daytime temperatures began to rise, though it was still freezing at night. One morning, they awoke to six inches of fresh snow, a reminder that it was still very much winter in the Adirondacks.

After breakfast, they gathered their fishing gear and headed to the lake.

Brad stayed at the edge of lake to build a fire. David and Jason trudged out onto the ice. David dragged a small, plastic sled bearing their fishing gear. He would do the fishing today. But Jason would help him get started.

About a hundred yards out, they stopped and lifted the augur from the sled. David held it up, the tip of the drill bit resting on the surface of the ice. Jason yanked the cord. The engine screamed to a start. David held the device steady and pressed a button on the handle.

The drill began spinning. It bit into the ice, sending pieces of ice flying. A few moments later, slushy water sloshed over the edges of the new hole.

David cut the engine. Jason helped him carry the augur back over to the sled, then headed back toward the edge of the lake.

He was about halfway to shore when he heard a noise, like muffled thunder, behind him. He felt a vibration beneath his feet.

He wheeled around. David was kneeling next to the hole, setting the tip-up. Crack! He dropped out of sight. A moment later, he popped up, like a bobber.

"Help!" he screamed, his bare fingers clawing at the edge of the ice.

Jason's instinct was to run toward him. But he froze, worried that he too might fall through.

At the edge of the lake, Brad saw what was happening.

"Jason!" he yelled. "Empty the sled and slide it over to David!"

Jason took a step toward the sled. But then he heard a loud crack and felt the ice beneath him shift and give way. Within seconds, he too was in the water.

Brad looked around for something he could use to pull his friends out. He spotted a long, thick pine bough on the ground. He grabbed it and ran out on to the ice.

He stopped about ten feet short of the open water. He lay down on his belly and inched forward, making sure the ice was secure, and slid the branch toward David.

"Grab it! I'll pull you out!"

David grabbed the branch with both hands. Brad got on his knees, leaned back and pulled as hard as he could. David was able to lift his elbows up onto the ice. But he could go no farther, and Brad was afraid to get too close to the edge of the ice.

Then David lurched forward. Jason was pushing him up from behind. His torso was now up on the ice. Only his legs still dangled in the water. Cautiously, Brad leaned forward, grabbed David by his coat and pulled him out.

Then he slid the branch back to the edge of the ice. Jason grabbed it and pulled himself up. Brad stood up and helped Jason to his feet. David was lying face down on the ice, moaning.

"Come on," Brad said, bending down on one knee. "Help me pick him up."

They put David's arms around their necks and dragged him toward the edge of the lake. It took them half an hour to get back to camp.

When they got there, David was mumbling incoherently. His lips were blue, and his fingers were white.

"Get into some dry clothes," Brad said to Jason. "I'll take care of him."

Brad unzipped David's tent and stuffed him inside. He laid him on his sleeping bag and peeled off his wet clothes. With a soft towel, he dried his skin, rubbing his arms and legs to warm them. He pulled clothes from his pack and dressed him in two layers.

He looked through David's gear but couldn't find another coat. So he went to his own tent and got his spare coat, along with a dry hat and pair of gloves, and put them on his friend.

Warming up, David began to come to his senses.

"What's going on?"

"You fell through the ice. But you're OK. Let's go out and sit by the fire."

By now, Jason had the fire roaring. Brad helped David sit down on a log, then sat beside him, propping him up.

"Thanks," David said, his teeth chattering.

"Yeah, thanks, Brad," Jason added.

"No problem, guys. I know you'd do the same for me."

...

An hour or so later, the three of them got so warm sitting around the fire that they took off their hats and gloves and unzipped their coats.

They'd been saving a bottle of bourbon for a special occasion. Falling through the ice and living to talk about it certainly seemed to qualify.

They sat around the fire, drinking, talking and even laughing about their ordeal the rest of the day.

And they kept talking, the rest of that winter and through the spring.

They shared everything. Their differences became plain. Once again, they argued.

But it didn't matter. They were friends. And the only thing that mattered was their friendship, which they'd let slip away until, one morning, it was put to a test.

The Box

He was on his way home from baseball practice when he spotted it between the Asher's garbage cans and the curb.

It was a wooden box, about two feet long, a foot and a half wide and a foot and a half deep. It had a brass handle on top, two brass latches on the front and three brass hinges on the back.

He skidded to a stop and hopped off his bike for a closer look. Squatting down, he flipped up the latches and pulled back the lid.

There was nothing inside except for a sheet of mottled, yellowed paper along the bottom. He closed the lid, refastened the latches and picked it up by the handle. It was heavy.

He'd been looking for a box to store some of his stuff. This one might do nicely, he thought.

He rode his bike home and walked back down the street to the Asher's. He felt a little funny taking it. But there it was, out on the curb on garbage night. Free game. He grabbed it and carried it home.

"What do you have there, Bobby?" his mother asked, as he lugged it through the back door.

"Just a box," he said, setting it down on the braided, wool rug in the center of the family room.

"Where'd you get it?"

"I found it out with the Asher's garbage."

"And you want to keep it?"

"Yeah."

"Why?"

"I want to put my stuff in it."

"What stuff?"

"My important stuff."

"Like what?"

"Well, like my ball glove and my baseball cards. You know, my important stuff."

"Let me have a look," his mother said, kneeling down beside it. Bobby got down on one knee next to her and opened it. His mother peeked inside.

"It's dirty. If you want to keep this, you're going to have to clean it first."

"Okay, Mom. What should I use?"

"Well, that looks like pretty good wood. Walnut, I think. I've got some wood soap. You can use that."

Bobby ripped the dingy paper from the bottom and scraped off several spots of crusty glue with a putty knife. Then he scrubbed the box inside and out. He even found some brass polish in the garage to shine up the fixtures.

His mother bought some blue felt to line the inside of the box. She helped him measure it, cut it and glue it to the bottom and the sides. His father applied a coat of varnish to the outside. Bobby was thrilled to see the wavy grain of the wood come to life.

Then he began gathering his treasures and carefully placing them inside. Beyond his ball glove and baseball cards, he put in his coin collection; a red, scale-model 1939 Chevy; a metal Band-Aid box with $7.26; a cast-iron cap gun; a Hershey bar; his Cub Scout handbook; his First Communion rosary; a geode he had found in Mammoth Cave; and a penny postcard his cousin Bill had mailed him from California.

Bobby's dad, who was in the printing business, made him a sticker that read: "Bobby's Most Important Things." Bobby happily affixed on top.

As he got older, the box got crowded, filling up with trophies and yearbooks. Bobby had to constantly rearrange things to make them fit.

He tried to wedge in his mortar board and diploma from his high school graduation, but they just wouldn't fit. So he jettisoned his baseball cards.

When he got married, he brought the box with him. He needed room for special gifts from his wife. So his cap gun and coin collection had to go.

Once he started a family, he had to lose his old ball glove and the 1939 Chevy to make room for his kids' drawings and their hand-made birthday and Father's Day cards.

He kept all his children's high school and college graduation programs. So his own diplomas had to go.

When he retired, he gave up his high school yearbooks to create a slot for an impressive plaque from his company.

When his first granddaughter was born, he carved out a new space for her pictures. Same with grandchildren number two, three and four. To make room, he ditched his retirement plaque.

He began to save Mass cards from his friends' funerals.

When his parents died, within a year of each other, he added their framed wedding picture. To make room, he gave up his last baseball trophy.

When his wife passed away, he got rid of everything but their wedding picture and her ring.

Then he scraped off the sticker his father had made for him so long ago. It was no longer legible anyway.

Now he is eighty-nine years old. He still has the box. The other day, he was showing it to his great granddaughter. He opened the lid, and she peeked inside.

"It's empty, Grandpa."

"I know. I've given everything away. Emma, would you like to have this box?"

"Oh, Grandpa! I'd love it! I have so many things I want to put in it."

Street Ball and Joe's Red Bike

On summer evenings, I used to watch my older brother Joe play football with his buddies in the street. I watched through our bedroom window on the second floor of our house. I was only five, and I wasn't allowed to play football with the older boys, especially in the street.

Theoretically, it was touch football. But it was rough, and someone would always get hurt. Guys would knock heads and skid across the pavement. Someone would trip up the curb or run into a telephone pole or a parked car. Once, Tom Clark tripped over a dog and broke his arm. It was not uncommon for some parent in our neighborhood to take his or her son to the emergency room because of injuries suffered during those games. One night, Joe broke his collar bone by running into a mailbox.

Inevitably, when someone got hurt, the moms would insist the boys move their game to the backyards. They would play back there, on the grass, for a night or two, then find their way back into the street, where injuries would resume.

I once asked Joe why they just didn't stay in the backyards.

"Too easy, kid," he said. "Too easy."

I idolized Joe. He was five years older than me. I admired so many things about him. He was smart. He was tall and handsome, with wavy blond hair and blue eyes. He played football, basketball, baseball, soccer and hockey and was a standout in every sport.

But the thing I admired most about Joe was that he was fearless. Nothing seemed to rattle him. I never saw him shrink from a challenge. He was the bravest person I've ever known.

"Life is risk," he would say, then plunge his bike down a hill so steep that the rest of us would never have thought of even walking it, let alone attempting it on our bikes.

That is until we saw Joe tear down it on his red Schwinn Phantom. We watched him barrel down the thin dirt trail, swerving to avoid rocks, bouncing over roots and ruts and narrowly missing trees. In awe, we watched him slam on his brake at the bottom, spinning his bike around.

"Come on down, you bastards!" he yelled, pumping his fists in the air.

Then, one by one, the rest of us would follow, riding our brakes the whole way.

All I did was try to imitate my big brother. At first, it wasn't easy. Taking risks didn't come naturally to me. I was okay playing football on the grass.

But the more I watched Joe and the more things I tried, the more I realized what I could do. When Joe became a teenager and pursued new interests, I even took his place leading the pack of footballers in the street.

...

I was thirteen when Joe enlisted in the Marines. It was 1968.

Dad knew he couldn't talk Joe out of signing up. He did try to convince him to join the Air Force instead. But that was like asking Joe to play football on the grass.

"I like the Marines, Dad," he said. "They're brave, and they take good care of each other."

He enlisted in March. Ten days later, he left for basic training. Joe and I said goodbye in the kitchen. Dad was taking him to the train station and, for some reason, I didn't go with them.

"Goodbye, kid," he said, hugging me tightly. We were not a family that hugged a lot, or even showed much emotion, and it felt strange to feel Joe's body so close to mine. But I loved it. I could feel how strong he had become.

"Will you write?" I asked.

"Oh, yeah," he said. "And you better write back."

"I will, Joe. I will."

Then he was gone. I remember my mom leaving the kitchen and going upstairs. I heard her bedroom door close, then heard her sobbing. I had never heard my mother cry. She did not stop crying or come out of her room until my father came home.

...

I got my first letter from Joe about two weeks later. He said basic training was the hardest thing he had ever done but he was "getting tough and ready for action."

He wrote me again a couple of times after that. He sounded so confident. It made me imagine him on his bike at the top of that hill, smiling and ready to take the plunge.

I wrote him back, proudly telling him I had made the Orioles in Babe Ruth League, his old team, and that I would be starting at second base, just like him.

In May, he shipped out to a place called Khe Sahn. Fierce battles had been raging there for months. For a while, the Americans were winning. But then the momentum shifted.

This was a strategic base, and the President ordered the military to hold it "at all costs." All branches stepped up, but the Marines were in the vanguard.

On his second day of combat, in a place known as Foxtrot Ridge, Joe's company was ambushed as it moved to support other Marines under fire. Joe was in the front line. He was killed as he was leading the way.

...

Joe was my only sibling. As the war raged on, my mother became terrified that I might be drafted. Then, just before I turned eighteen, the war came to an end.

I was attending an all-boys Catholic high school. On the day the peace accords were signed, Father Lorean asked for volunteers to ring the bell in the church steeple. I was the first to raise my hand.

He recruited twelve of us. He told us to line up, single file, up the narrow steps to the belfry, where each of us would pull on the rope for one minute. Twelve minutes for twelve years of U.S. involvement in the war. I made sure I was seventh in line. I wanted to mark the seventh year of the war, 1968, the deadliest year, the year my brother was taken away.

When my turn came, I grabbed the rope and pulled it hard, with all my strength. All I could think of was Joe. I pulled and I pulled and I pulled until Father Lorean grabbed my arm and told me it was time. I gave up the rope and fell to my knees, sobbing, my head at Father Lorean's feet, as the bell continued to toll.

...

When I got home that afternoon, I changed clothes, opened the garage door, pulled out Joe's bike and took off down the street.

I rode to the edge of town, to the place where Joe used to take his bike down the big hill. I stopped and stood there, straddling the bike, and looked over the edge. It looked even steeper than I remembered it.

I drew a breath, squeezed the hand grips and pushed off over the edge. The bike bounced violently on the rocky trail. About twenty-five yards down, I flew off and landed in some tall grass. Fortunately, I was okay.

I got back on Joe's bike and kept going. Another fifty yards down, the front tire hit a big root. I popped off and landed on my back.

Lying there, with the wind knocked out of me, I thought about giving up. But then I heard a voice. "Too easy, kid." I got back on.

Another fifty yards down, the front tire hit a deep rut, and I flew off again, this time over the handlebars. I hit the ground hard but rolled. Again, I was okay.

Joe's bike wasn't so lucky. The front rim was bent. I rocked the bike back and forth. It wobbled. But at this point, I was close to the bottom. So I got back on and rode the brake the rest of the way. The bike shook badly, but it held up.

I made it. I remembered Joe being in this very spot, pumping his fists in the air. Now I looked up and raised my arms toward heaven.

Then I got off and walked Joe's bike over to a patch of grass. I laid it down and knelt beside it.

"Goodbye, Joe," I said, touching the sturdy frame one last time.

Author's Note

When I retired, after working for 31 years in public relations at Procter & Gamble, I wasn't sure exactly what to do next. Upon retiring, many professionals go into consulting. But I wanted to do something new.

I remembered running into one of our retired executives a few years earlier. I'd worked with him closely. He was one of the most anxious guys I'd ever known. I never saw him without a cup of coffee, a cigarette and a furrowed brow.

Now, though, he looked completely relaxed. He was fit, tan and looked about twenty years younger. I asked him what he was doing these days.

He told me that, after he retired, he didn't know what to do. "I just sat on my front porch for about six weeks and thought deeply about what I loved doing as a young man." As it turned out, for him, that was scuba diving. He had decided to become a scuba diving instructor and was now spending about six months of the year in the Caribbean.

"Think about your original interests," he told me, "the things you've put on hold for years, the things that once lit you up."

Eventually, those original interests resurfaced for me.

One was teaching. I'm now in my fourth year of teaching public relations at my alma mater, Xavier University in Cincinnati. I love it.

Another was writing creatively. I was an English major in college. But I had to go to a week-long writing workshop in New Harmony, Indiana in June of 2014 to begin to learn how to write creatively again. Three decades of memo writing had done wonders for my efficiency but just about killed my creativity. I had to start over. After the workshop, I began writing short stories and essays and getting them published.

Get Back is a collection of twelve of these stories. It is my first book. Writing these stories has been the result of my own journey back to one of my original interests. My new interests turned out to be my old interests.

I share this as an invitation to rediscover your original interests, to find your way back, to reconnect with your true self. No matter where you are, it is not too late, and it will light you up.

Don Tassone
February 2017